MAIN ABIJA
MY GRANDAD

KAREN ROGERS

ALLEN&UNWIN
SYDNEY • MELBOURNE • AUCKLAND • LONDON

Bla main biginini, gagumob, bla main lilwan
dedi en bla ola Rogers femili

For my children, grandchildren,
my great-grandson and the Rogers family

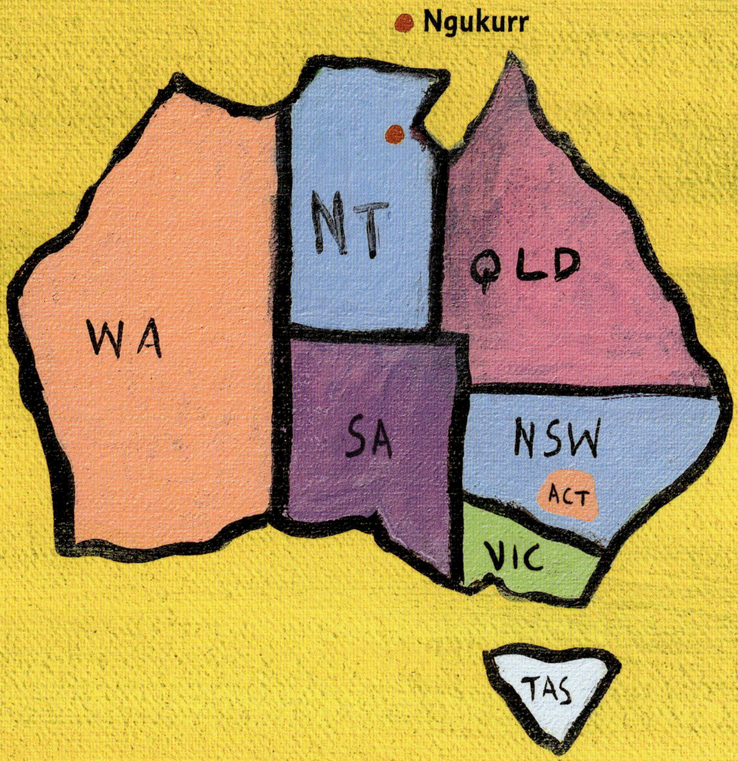

My home is Ngukurr in the Northern Territory.

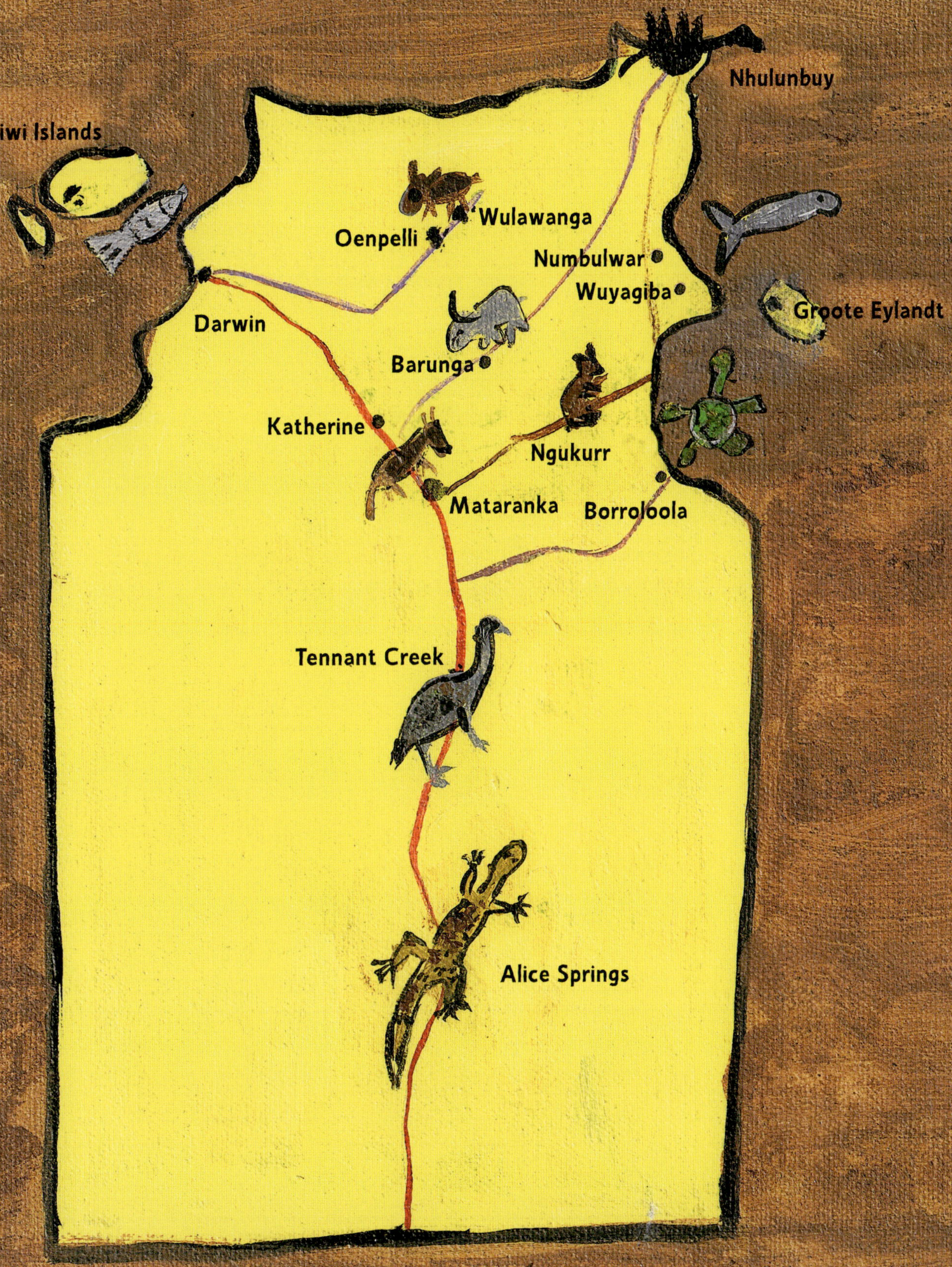

Mi oldei jinggibat det skul holidei la Wuyagiba
wen ai bin lilgel. Wuyagiba im bla main abija
kantri gulijap la solwada.

I remember the times I spent my school holidays
in Wuyagiba when I was a little girl. Wuyagiba is
my grandad's outstation, near the saltwater.

Mela oldei gu fishing en swiming garra det trupi.
Main abija oldei sing garra langgus, en imin dali mela
ba hu drimin en ba hu kantri than.

We went fishing and swimming in that troopy.
Grandad sang in language and he explained whose
Dreaming was there and which Country it belonged to.

Det olmen im oldei titjim mela det koltja wei.

That old man taught me and my family cultural ways.

Imin titjim mi bla faindi shugabeg. Bla faindi shugabeg, yu garra luk bla det shugabeg hanibi ontop la tri o andanith la rok. Main abija bin titjim mi bla katim en splitim det tri bla digimat det shugabeg.

He taught me how to find sugarbag. You need to look for the sugarbag honey bees up in the trees or under the rocks. My grandad also taught me how to cut the tree and split it in half to get the sugarbag honey out.

Ai bin im feibritwan.

I was his favourite.

Wen mela bin gu hanting main abija bin garrimap mi la im nek.

When we went hunting Grandad carried me on his neck.

Ai gin stil jinggibat im feis hau im oldei lukap la mi en smail wen ai holdi im hen.

I remember his face and that happy expression when I was hanging on to his hands.

Det olmen bin gromap mi wen main
mami bin sik en gu la Darwin.

That old man grew me up when my mother
got sick and went to Darwin.

Ai bin lilwan.

I was five or six years old.

Det olmen imin stokmen en imin serimoni men.

Grandad worked as a stockman and was a well-respected cultural leader.

Imin abu waitwan hos neim Apple Eater.

He had a white horse named Apple Eater.

Mela bin oldei bulrum im wen imin oldei jidan la stok kemp. Ai garri mak la main leig, im meigi mi jinggibat Wulawanga steishin gulijap la Oenpelli.

We followed him around as kids, staying at the stock camps. I've got a mark on my leg that reminds me of Wulawanga station, near Oenpelli.

Wen main abija en gagu bin libu mijel, main abija
bin gu jidan la Numbulwar.

When my grandma and grandad broke up,
my grandad moved to live at Numbulwar.

Mela bin gu luk im bat samtaims
det toyoda bin nugud.

We would visit him but sometimes
the troopy would break down.

Wen ai bin growap en ai bin abu main oun femili, main lilwan dota Karissa bin jidan wan manth gada main abija. Imin titjim main dota hau ba hant, fish en ba gajim shugabeg, laik imin tijtim mi. Imin gibit main dota en san blekbala neim.

When I grew up and had a family of my own, my youngest daughter, Karissa, spent one month with my grandad. He taught her how to hunt, fish and collect sugarbag, just as he had with me. He also gave my daughter and son bush names.

Wen main abija bin olmen, ai bin oldei gu luk la im la Numbulwar wen ai bin abu breik burru wek.

As my grandad got old, I would visit him in Numbulwar when I had a break from work.

Ai bin sed en enggri wen main abija bin finish.
Ai nomo bin ja, ibin bla im fyunrul. Ai bin longwei la Darwin.

I was sad and angry when my grandad passed away.
I wasn't there, even for his funeral.
I was a long way away in Darwin.

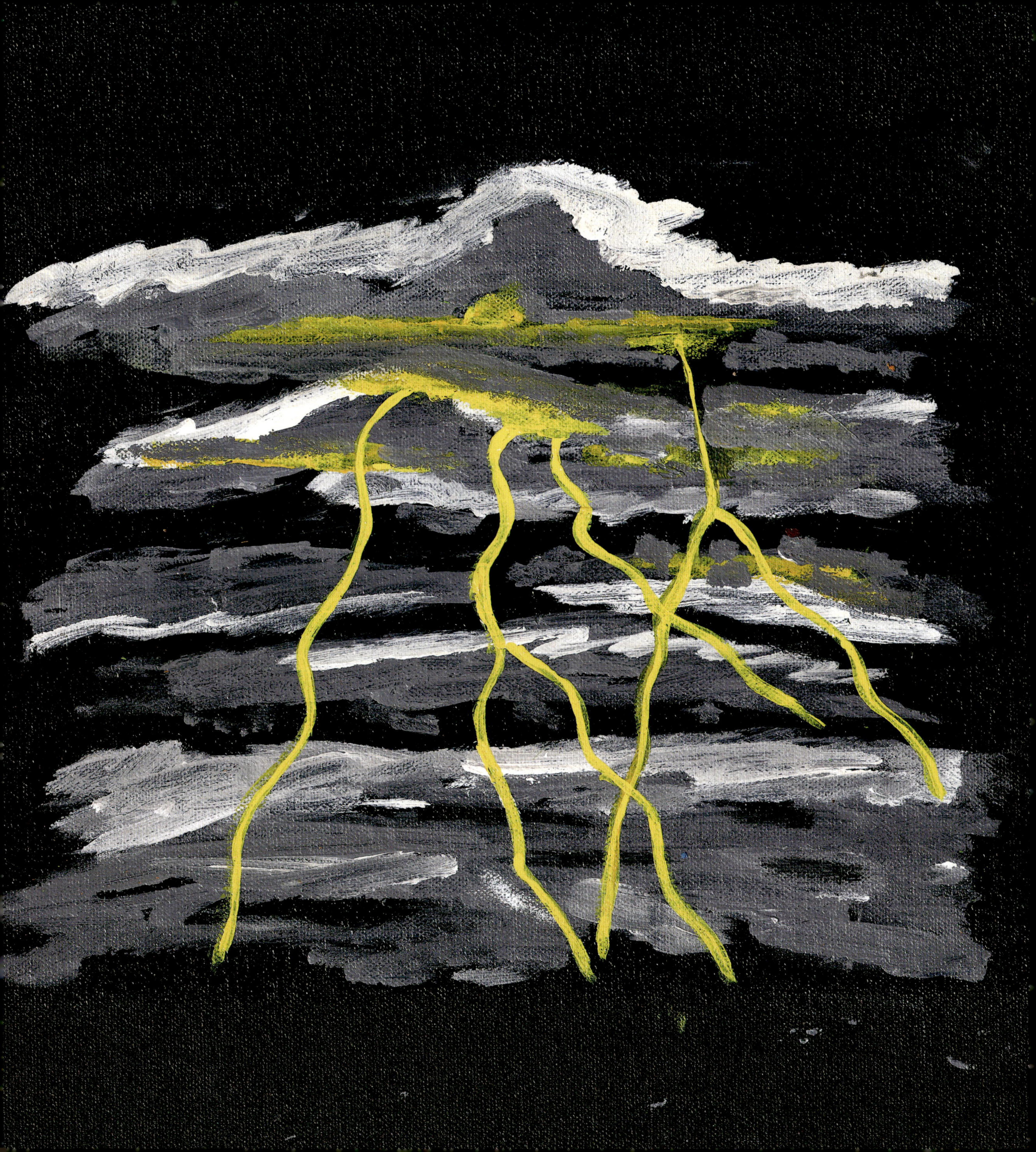

Mi mis main abija, bat mi gadi main gagumob en main lilwan dedi na. Wani main abija bin du ba main, ai gin dum gada main gagumob en main lilwan dedi.

I really miss my old grandad, but now I'm a grandmother and a great-grandmother, I can do for my grandkids what he did for me.

Main lilwan dedi leigi fishing en im
oldei tok 'ish, ish'.

My great-grandson loves fishing too.
'Ish, ish,' he says.

Mi garri la gabarra wani main abija bin tijtim mi en mi dalimbat main biginini en gagumob.

I remember everything my grandad taught me and I am now passing it on to my children and grandkids.

Photo by Helen Orr

Mi burru Ropa Riba – Ngukurr. Main atwek im burru main koltjurul nolij en main filing ba dis kantri.

Mi jidan gada main femili la Ngukurr. Ai garri faib biginini, eit gagumob en wanbala dedi. Ai bin stadi la Batchelor, inspaiyid burru main gagu en im sistamob hu bin ol atis. Ai wek gada tekstail, glas en kenbis, en mi dumbat enimeishin du. Ai laigi lenlen nyu skils en olkain staiyil. La 2018, ai bin dum residinsi la Canberra en la 2020 ai bin gedim Kriyeitib Felouship burru Arts NT.

Main Abija, im main fes pitja buk.

I come from Ngukurr Community in South East Arnhem Land in the Northern Territory. My artwork comes from cultural knowledge and my feelings for the land.

I live with my family at Ngukurr. I have five children, eight grandkids and one great-grandson. I studied Visual Arts at Batchelor Institute, inspired by my grandmother and her sisters, who were all artists. I work with textiles, glass and canvas and am currently working on an animation. I love learning new skills and different art forms. In 2018 I was an artist in residence at Glassworks, Canberra and in 2020 I received a Creative Fellowship from Arts NT.

Main Abija My Grandad is my first picture book.

Bla irrim Karen ridrid dijan buk gada Kriol en Ingglish, skenim dijan QR Koud gada yu fon, o gu la det websait: www.allenandunwin.com/main-abija

To listen to Karen reading this book in Kriol and English, please scan the QR code, or go to www.allenandunwin.com/main-abija

STORY PROJECTS

This book was developed during the 2019 Octopus Story Camp in Darwin, facilitated by Johanna Bell and Erica Wagner

With thanks to Johanna Bell, Erica Wagner, Craig Smith and Jo Hunt for their enthusiasm and expertise. Thanks to linguists Jackie van den Boss and Greg Dickson for help with Kriol translations. Thanks to Jude Emmett from Ngukurr Art Centre and Courtney Collins from Ngukurr Story Project for their support. Thanks to Elise Jones and Davina Bell from Allen & Unwin. And always, thanks to my family.

First published by Allen & Unwin in 2021

Allen & Unwin
83 Alexander Street
Crows Nest NSW 2065
Australia
Phone: (61 2) 8425 0100
Email: info@allenandunwin.com
Web: www.allenandunwin.com

NATIONAL LIBRARY OF AUSTRALIA
A catalogue record for this book is available from the National Library of Australia

ISBN 978 1 76052 603 0

For teaching resources, explore www.allenandunwin.com/resources/for-teachers

Illustration technique: acrylic on canvas

Cover and text design by Joanna Hunt
Author photo by Helen Orr, 2019
Set in 15pt Emory by Joanna Hunt
Colour reproduction by Splitting Image, Clayton, Victoria
Printed in November 2020 by Hang Tai Printing Company Limited, China

1 3 5 7 9 10 8 6 4 2

FSC www.fsc.org
MIX
Paper from responsible sources
FSC® C023121

ngukurrarts.com/artist/karen-rogers/